D1582627

Sleepytime
Stories
and
Rhymes

Stories re-told by Maureen Spurgeon

Brown Watson
ENGLAND

HEY DIDDLE, DIDDLE

Hey diddle, diddle,
The cat and the fiddle,
The cow jumped over the moon.

2

The little dog laughed
To see such sport,
And the dish ran away with the spoon.

WEE WILLIE WINKIE

Wee Willie Winkie
Runs through the town,
Upstairs and downstairs
In his nightgown.

4

Rapping at the window,
Crying through the lock,
Are the children all in bed,
For it's past eight o'clock?

5

MARY, MARY

Mary, Mary, quite contrary,
How does your garden grow?
With silver bells and cockle shells
And pretty maids all in a row.

SEE-SAW MARGERY DAW

See-saw Margery Daw,
Johnny shall have a new master;
He shall have but a penny a day,
Because he can't work any faster.

7

ONE, TWO, BUCKLE MY SHOE

One, two, buckle my shoe;
Three, four, knock at the door;
Five, six, pick up sticks;
Seven, eight, lay them straight;

Nine, ten, my fat hen;

Eleven, twelve,
dig and delve.

SING A SONG OF SIXPENCE

Sing a song of sixpence,
A pocket full of rye;
Four and twenty blackbirds
Baked in a pie.

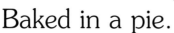

When the pie was opened,
The birds began to sing;
Wasn't that a dainty dish
To set before the King.

The King was in his counting house
Counting out his money;
The Queen was in the parlour
Eating bread and honey.

The maid was in the garden
Hanging out the clothes;
When down came a blackbird
And pecked off her nose.

13

DOCTOR FOSTER

Doctor Foster went to Gloucester
In a shower of rain;
He stepped in a puddle,
Right up to his middle,
And never went there again.

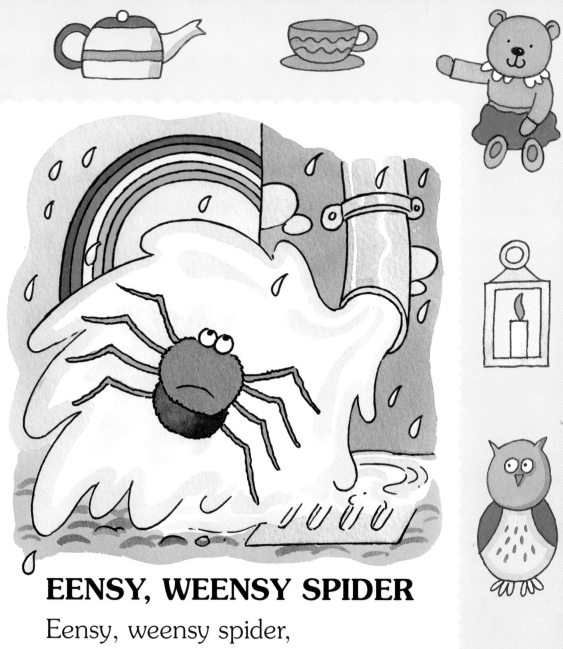

EENSY, WEENSY SPIDER

Eensy, weensy spider,
Climbed the water spout.
Down came the rain
And washed the spider out.

15

HOT CROSS BUNS

Hot cross buns!
Hot cross buns!
One a penny,
Two a penny,
Hot cross buns!

16

If you have no daughters,
Give them to your sons.
One a penny,
Two a penny,
Hot cross buns!

LITTLE BO-PEEP

Little Bo-Peep has lost her sheep,
And doesn't know where to find them;

18

Leave them alone,
And they'll come home,
Wagging their tails behind them.

19

Snow White

Long ago, a queen sat sewing at a
palace window. Looking out at the
white snow drifting against the
black window frame, she pricked
her finger and three drops of blood
fell. "If only I had a daughter with
skin as white as snow, blood-red
cheeks and hair as black as the
window frame," she sighed, "I
would call her Snow White."

Before long, the queen's wish was granted. Everyone celebrated the birth of her baby daughter. And, as the years passed, Snow White became more and more beautiful.

But the happy times were not to last. Suddenly, the good queen became ill and died. Within a year, Snow White's father had taken another wife, as hard-hearted as she was beautiful.

23

The new queen was also very vain. Her greatest treasure was a magic mirror. Every day she asked it the same question. "Mirror, mirror on the wall, who is the fairest one of all?"

24

The answer from the magic
mirror was always the same.
"In all the land,
'Tis thou, oh queen!
Thou art the fairest
To be seen!"

Then, one day, the mirror gave a different answer.
"No maiden was more fair than thou! But Snow White is the fairest, now!"

The queen flew into a terrible rage,
screaming for a palace guard.
"Take Snow White into the forest!"
she stormed. "Put her to death!
Then bring me back her heart!"

27

The guard was shocked. He knew he had to do as the queen said. But, by the time he and Snow White reached the forest, he had made up his mind that he could never do such a wicked deed.

He told her of the danger she was in. "Run away, as far as you can," he begged Snow White, "so the queen will not find you! I shall take back a deer's heart and pretend it is yours!"

Snow White wandered through
the forest until she found a little
cottage.

"Anyone at home?" she called,
stepping inside, but nobody
answered.

The cottage was very dusty and Snow White soon set to work and tidied up.

"I wonder who lives here?" she thought, dusting the seven little chairs set around the table.

By the time she had washed up
and made the seven little beds,
Snow White was feeling tired. She
slept, and awoke to see seven
little faces looking down on her.

When the seven little dwarfs heard Snow White's story, they made her promise she would stay with them and not open the door to anyone! Snow White promised.

At that very moment, the magic mirror was telling the queen, "In the seven dwarfs' cottage, Snow White lives now. She is, dear queen, still fairer than thou!"

The queen went white with rage!
Determined to put an end to
Snow White, she disguised herself
as an old pedlar woman, then put
poison into the rosiest apple she
could find…

35

With her magic powers, the queen soon found the cottage in the forest and tapped at the door. "Lovely apples!" she croaked, as Snow White came to the window. "Try one, my dear."

Snow White did not want to hurt an old woman's feelings. One bite of the poisoned apple and she fell to the floor. Cackles of wild laughter from the wicked queen echoed all through the forest.

The dwarfs were heartbroken when they found dear Snow White. Wanting to keep her with them for ever, they put her in a crystal casket and set it down in her favourite part of the forest.

As time passed, the story of the beautiful young princess asleep in a crystal casket began to spread. One day, a handsome young prince decided to discover the truth for himself.

The moment he saw Snow White, he had to lean over and kiss her. Her eyelids fluttered, and as she looked into the face of the young prince, she knew she loved him as much as he already loved her.

Very soon, the dwarfs were invited to Snow White's wedding. When the wicked queen heard the news, she got into such a temper that she disappeared in a big puff of smoke!

ROCK-A-BYE BABY

Rock-a-bye baby,
On the tree top,
When the wind blows
The cradle will rock.

When the bough breaks,
The cradle will fall –
Down will come baby,
Cradle and all!

THIS LITTLE PIGGY

This little piggy went to market,
This little piggy stayed at home,
This little piggy had roast beef,
This little piggy had none,
And this little piggy cried,
"Wee, wee, wee," all the way home!

TO BED, TO BED

"To bed, to bed!" said Sleepy Head.
"Tarry a while," said Slow.
"Put on the pan," said Greedy Ann.
"We'll sup before we go."

MARY HAD A LITTLE LAMB

Mary had a little lamb,
Its fleece was white as snow,
And everywhere that Mary went
That lamb was sure to go.

46

It followed her to school one day,
That was against the rule;
It made the children laugh and play,
To see a lamb at school.

JACK SPRAT

Jack Sprat could eat no fat,
His wife could eat no lean,
And so between them both,
They licked the platter clean.

48

Jack ate all the lean,
Joan ate all the fat,
The bone they picked it clean,
Then gave it to the cat.

49

LITTLE POLLY FLINDERS

Little Polly Flinders
Sat among the cinders,
Warming her pretty little toes;

50

Her mother came and caught her,
And whipped her little daughter
For spoiling her nice new clothes.

PAT-A-CAKE

Pat-a-cake, pat-a-cake, baker's man,
Bake me a cake as fast as you can;
Pat it and prick it and mark it with B,
And put it in the oven for baby and me.

52

TOMMY TUCKER

Little Tommy Tucker
Sang for his supper;
What shall we give him?
White bread and butter.
How shall he cut it without any knife?
How will he marry, without any wife?

53

LITTLE BOY BLUE

Little Boy Blue,
Come blow your horn,
The sheep's in the meadow,
The cow's in the corn.

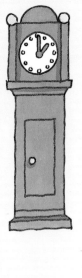

54

Where is the boy
Who looks after the sheep?
He's under the haystack,
Fast asleep!

HALF A POUND OF TUPPENNY RICE

Half a pound of tuppenny rice,
Half a pound of treacle,
That's the way the money goes,
Pop goes the weasel!

Up and down the city road,
In and out the Eagle,
That's the way the money goes,
Pop goes the weasel!

THERE WAS A CROOKED MAN

There was a crooked man,
And he walked a crooked mile,
He found a crooked sixpence
Against a crooked stile;

58

He bought a crooked cat,
Which caught a crooked mouse,
And they all lived together
In a little crooked house.

Cinderella

Once, Cinderella and her father, the Baron, had lived alone, after the death of her mother when she was a baby. How she sighed, remembering those happy days before her father married a widow with two daughters of her own.

61

The widow's daughters were so ugly and cruel, they quickly became known as The Ugly Sisters.

Soon, the Baron's daughter was made to do all the housework.

She was dressed in rags, and
because she spent so much time
in the kitchen among the cinders,
they called her "Cinderella".

Then, one morning, Cinderella heard a loud knock at the door. It was a message from the royal palace, sent to all the houses in the kingdom.

"Invitations to a Grand Ball in
honour of the Prince Charming"
squealed the Ugly Sisters.
Cinderella's heart began to beat.

Cinderella soon realised she would not be allowed to go to the Ball. The Ugly Sisters made her alter their dresses and polish their shoes.

By the evening of the Ball,
Cinderella was very unhappy.
Then, suddenly, their was a flash
of light and a stranger appeared
before her.

"Who are you?" Cinderella said, looking at the stranger.
"Your Fairy Godmother," came the reply. "And with my magic wand, I shall see that you go to the Ball!"

Before Cinderella could answer, her Fairy Godmother gave a tap with her wand. In an instant, her rags became the most beautiful ball gown she could ever have imagined!

"I shall need a pumpkin..." said the Fairy Godmother. "There's one in the kitchen garden..." said Cinderella.

70

The Fairy Godmother
turned a fat pumpkin into a
crystal coach! Four mice
became white ponies, and two
rats were changed into footmen!

"Thank you, Fairy Godmother!"
cried Cinderella.
"Just remember! My magic can
only last until midnight!" her Fairy
Godmother smiled.

Well, what a stir when Cinderella arrived at the Palace! Everyone wanted to know who the pretty young girl was. Even Prince Charming came straight up to talk to her.

They danced the whole evening,
falling in love with each hour that
slipped by. The Ugly Sisters had
no idea that the beautiful girl was
Cinderella!

74

On the first stroke of midnight,
Cinderella remembered what her
Fairy Godmother had said.
"I - I have to go!" she cried, and
turned to run down the stairs.

Prince Charming was surprised and knew he had to see the beautiful girl again. The only clue she left was a tiny, glass slipper...

There was great excitement next day. A royal procession came around all the streets, with a page carrying the glass slipper on a pink cushion.

"Whoever this slipper fits," said
the Royal Herald, "shall marry
Prince Charming!"
"It will fit me!" squealed the first
Ugly Sister. "It will fit me!"

78

"No, me!" screamed her sister. But, the slipper was much too small for either of them.

"But, this is the last house!" cried the Herald. "Is there nobody else?"

"Only my daughter," said the Baron quickly. "I'll call her." And even before he put the slipper on Cinderella's tiny foot, the Prince knew she was the girl he loved.

Cinderella and Prince Charming
soon celebrated their marriage.
And somewhere, Cinderella
knew, her Fairy Godmother was
there, smiling.

81

TOM THE PIPER'S SON

Tom, Tom, the piper's son,
Stole a pig and away did run;
The pig was eat and Tom was beat,
And Tom went howling down the street.

COBBLER, COBBLER

Cobbler, cobbler, mend my shoe,
Get it done by half-past-two;
Stitch it up and stitch it down,
Then I'll give you half-a-crown.

LADYBIRD, LADYBIRD

Ladybird, ladybird,
Fly away home.
Your house is on fire,
Your children are gone;

84

All except one,
And that's little Ann,
And she crept under
The warming pan.

HUMPTY DUMPTY

Humpty Dumpty sat on a wall,
Humpty Dumpty had a great fall.

All the King's horses
And all the King's men,
Couldn't put Humpty together again.

ROUND AND ROUND
THE GARDEN

Round and round the garden
Like a teddy bear.
One step, two steps,
Tickle me under there.

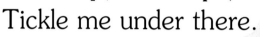

Round and round the haystack
Went the little mouse.
One step, two steps,
In his little house.

RING-A-RING O'ROSES

Ring-a-ring o'roses,
A pocket full of posies,
A-tishoo! A-tishoo!
We all fall down.

TWINKLE, TWINKLE, LITTLE STAR

Twinkle, twinkle, little star,
How I wonder what you are!
Up above the world so high,
Like a diamond in the sky.

DING, DONG, BELL

Ding, dong, bell,
Pussy's in the well.
Who put her in?
Little Johnny Thin.

Who pulled her out?
Little Tommy Stout.
What a naughty boy was that
To try to drown poor pussycat,
Who never did him any harm,
But killed all the mice
In his father's barn.

93

GOOSEY GANDER

Goosey, goosey gander,
Where shall I wander?
Upstairs and downstairs,
In my lady's chamber.

94

Where I met an old man,
Who wouldn't say his prayers,
I took him by the left leg,
And threw him down the stairs.

PUSSY CAT, PUSSY CAT

Pussy cat, pussy cat,
Where have you been?
I've been up to London,
To visit the Queen.

Pussy cat, pussy cat,
What did you there?
I frightened a little mouse,
Under a chair.

LITTLE JACK HORNER

Little Jack Horner sat in a corner,
Eating his Christmas pie;
He put in his thumb,
And pulled out a plum,
And said "What a good boy am I!"

COCK-A-DOODLE DOO!

Cock-a-doodle doo!
My dame has lost her shoe,
My master's lost his fiddling stick,
And knows not what to do.

W. RABBIT

Alice in Wonderland

Alice was tired of sitting on the bank. The sun made her feel sleepy. She was wondering about making a daisy chain, when a white rabbit ran past saying, "Oh, dear! Oh, dear! I shall be too late!" He took a watch from his waistcoat pocket!

Alice had never seen a white rabbit
with a waistcoat, or a pocket
watch, so she followed him to see
where he was going. When the
White Rabbit went down a rabbit
hole – down went Alice after it.

W. RABBIT

Suddenly, Alice felt herself falling. She landed on a heap of dry leaves. "Oh dear," she heard the White Rabbit saying, "how late it is getting!"

All at once, he vanished from sight, leaving Alice in a long, low hall with locked doors all around. Alice came across a little table on which there was a key. But, which door did it fit?

W. RABBIT

Then she came across a tiny door behind a curtain. She turned the key in the lock and the door opened. Kneeling down, she could see a beautiful garden, with bright flower beds and water fountains.

"Now," thought Alice, "how do I get out?" On the table where the key had been, there was a bottle with "DRINK ME!" written on a label around the neck. It was the most delicious drink Alice had ever tasted!

W. RABBIT

DRINK ME

And with every drop, Alice
became smaller and smaller. Soon,
she was just the right size to get
through the little door and into the
beautiful garden. If only she had
not left the key on the table…

Then, she found a box with a cake inside. In currants were the words, "EAT ME." So Alice did, growing taller and taller. Soon she was much too big to go through the door, even though she had the key!

W. RABBIT

Alice was so sad, she began to cry. Before long, there was the patter of feet and in came the White Rabbit. The sight of such a big, tall Alice frightened him so much, he dropped the fan and gloves he was carrying.

Alice picked up the fan, quickly dropping it when she found herself shrinking again! Her foot slipped, and – splash! She was up to her chin in the pool of tears she had wept when she had been so big and tall.

In the pool of tears was also a
duck, a dodo and a mouse who
told a story to get everyone dry!
"Mary Ann!" called a voice.
"Fetch me my gloves this
minute!" It was the White Rabbit.

This time, Alice followed him to a little house with "W. RABBIT" on the door. Coming out the other side, she saw a huge mushroom, about as tall as she was now, on which a caterpillar sat, smoking a pipe!

112

The caterpillar said that eating one side of the mushroom would make her taller, the other side, smaller. So Alice took a piece of each. A Cheshire Cat grinned at her from a tree.

"Please," said Alice to the cat, "which was should I go?"
"That way," said the cat waving his right paw, "lives the Mad Hatter, and that way," waving his other paw, "lives the March Hare!"

W. RABBIT

The March Hare's house had a roof thatched with fur and chimneys shaped like long ears! He and the Mad Hatter sat outside at a table, resting their elbows on a very sleepy little dormouse.

"Tell us a story!" ordered the March Hare.

"Well," said Alice, taken by surprise, "I don't think…"

"Don't think?" he echoed. "Then you shouldn't talk!"

116

That was enough to make Alice
march away from the table. Quite
by chance she saw one of the trees
had a door set in it. When Alice
opened it, she was in the hall again.

Nibbling one side of the caterpillar's mushroom, then the other, Alice made herself the right size to get the key. She went through the little door and out into the beautiful garden, at last!

Here, two gardeners were painting white roses red! "We planted a white rose by mistake!" explained one, "and if the queen finds out…Oh no! Here she comes now!"

119

The Queen of Hearts stopped when she saw Alice. "What is your name, child?" she asked. "My name," said Alice, "is Alice." "Can you play croquet?" "Oh, yes!" cried Alice.

W. RABBIT

Alice had never played croquet using flamingoes to hit curled-up hedgehogs! Before long the game was a real mess, with the queen yelling "Off with his head!" every other minute.

Suddenly, the cry went up,
"The trial is beginning!"
"What trial?" asked Alice – but
everyone was already running
ahead, carrying her along with
them into a big court room.

122

"The charge is," said the White
Rabbit, "that the Knave of Hearts
stole some tarts!"

"Call the first witness!" said the
king. And to her great surprise,
the White Rabbit called, "Alice!"

"What do you know of this?"
asked the king.
"Nothing whatsoever," said Alice.
"Off with her head!" shouted the
Queen of Hearts, red in the face.
"You?" went on Alice. "You're
only a pack of cards!"

124

At once, the cards rose up and
came flying down on her! Alice
gave a little scream and found
herself back on the bank.
Her adventures in Wonderland
had only been a wonderful dream!

BAA, BAA, BLACK SHEEP

Baa, baa, black sheep,
Have you any wool?
Yes, sir, yes, sir,
Three bags full.

One for the master,
And one for the dame,
And one for the little boy
Who lives down the lane.

I'M A LITTLE TEAPOT

I'm a little teapot,
Short and stout,
Here's my handle,
Here's my spout.

128

When I see the teacups,
Hear me shout:
Tip me up and pour me out!

THE QUEEN OF HEARTS

The Queen of Hearts
She made some tarts,
All on a summer's day;
The Knave of Hearts
He stole the tarts,
And took them right away.

The King of Hearts
Called for the tarts,
And beat the Knave full sore;
The Knave of Hearts
Brought back the tarts,
And vowed he'd steal no more.

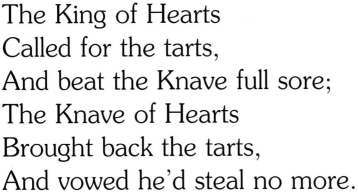

RAIN, RAIN, GO AWAY

Rain, rain, go away,
Come back another day,
All the children want to play.
Rain, rain, go to Spain,
Never show your face again.

IT'S RAINING,
IT'S POURING

It's raining, it's pouring,
The old man is snoring.
He went to bed
And bumped his head,
And couldn't get up in the morning!

133

CURLY LOCKS

Curly Locks, Curly Locks,
Will you be mine?
You shall not wash dishes,
Nor yet feed the swine;

You'll sit on a cushion
And sew a fine seam,
And feed upon strawberries,
Sugar and cream.

POLLY PUT THE KETTLE ON

Polly put the kettle on,
Polly put the kettle on,
Polly put the kettle on,
We'll all have tea.

Sukey take it off again,
Sukey take it off again,
Sukey take it off again,
They've all gone away.

137

OLD KING COLE

Old King Cole was a merry old soul,
And a merry old soul was he;

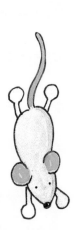

He called for his pipe,
And he called for his bowl,
And he called for his fiddlers three.

139

LITTLE MISS MUFFET

Little Miss Muffet
Sat on her tuffet,
Eating her curds and whey;
There came a big spider,
Who sat down beside her,
And frightened Miss Muffet away.

140

JACK AND JILL

Jack and Jill went up the hill,
To fetch a pail of water;
Jack fell down and broke his crown,
And Jill came tumbling after.

RUB-A-DUB-DUB

Rub-a-dub-dub,
Three men in a tub,
And who do you think they be?

142

The butcher, the baker,
The candlestick-maker,
And up they jump all three!

Sleeping Beauty

There was once a king and queen
who seemed to have everything
that anyone could possibly want.
They had a lovely palace, huge
estates, and all the people in the
kingdom loved them. Yet, still
they longed for just one thing
more – a child of their own.

After many a sad and lonely year, a beautiful baby daughter was born. The king and queen were happier than they had ever been.

"We shall give a party to celebrate," announced the king. "And all the fairies shall be invited!" cried the queen.

So the invitations were written,
ready for birds to take them to all
parts of the kingdom. Nobody
saw one invitation fluttering down
into the lake...

It was the invitation for the Fairy Carabos.

When she heard there was to be a royal party, which she was not invited to, she was furious!

149

She ran to the palace, where
the other fairies were gathered
around the cradle, ready to bless
the royal baby with gifts of
kindness, happiness and beauty.

150

"Hah!" screamed a cruel, mocking voice. "Heed the spell of Carabos! On her fifteenth birthday, the princess will prick her finger on a spindle, and die!"

151

With a wild cackle of laughter
which rang all round the palace,
Carabos swept out. She nodded
her head in satisfaction to hear
the gasps of horror behind her.

The fairies knew Carabos was far
more powerful than them.
"But, perhaps," one said at last,
"we can put our magic together
and change the spell, just a little…"

153

"It means the princess will sleep for a hundred years when she pricks her finger. She will not die," she told the worried parents.

"All the spindles in the kingdom must be broken to keep our child safe!" cried the king.

Soon the evil spell was forgotten.

On her fifteenth
birthday, the princess
wandered through the
palace gardens and found a
little door she had never
seen before.

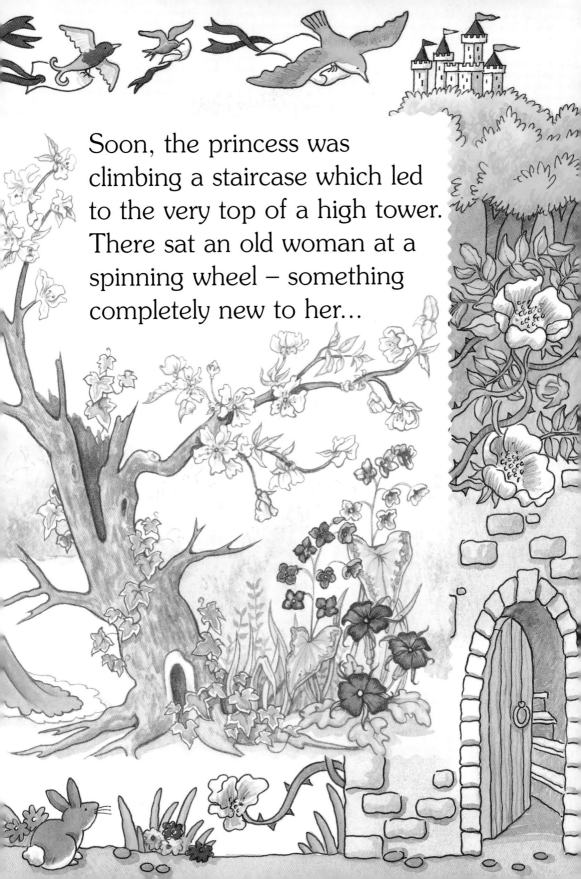

Soon, the princess was climbing a staircase which led to the very top of a high tower. There sat an old woman at a spinning wheel – something completely new to her...

"Come, learn to spin, my dear," cackled the old woman. "Just take the spindle..." And in one terrible instant, the wicked spell of Carabos came true!

The beautiful young princess pricked her finger and fell to the ground. Soon, even the wild screams of laughter from Carabos faded into complete silence.

Throughout the kingdom, nothing moved. The grass, the bushes and hedges around the palace grew tall and thick.

The story of the Sleeping Beauty became a legend, a tale which parents told their children. Until, one day, a brave prince decided to try and discover the truth...

On and on he rode, until he came to the forest, so thick and dark, there seemed no way in. But, as he raised his sword to cut through the greenery, a strange thing happened...

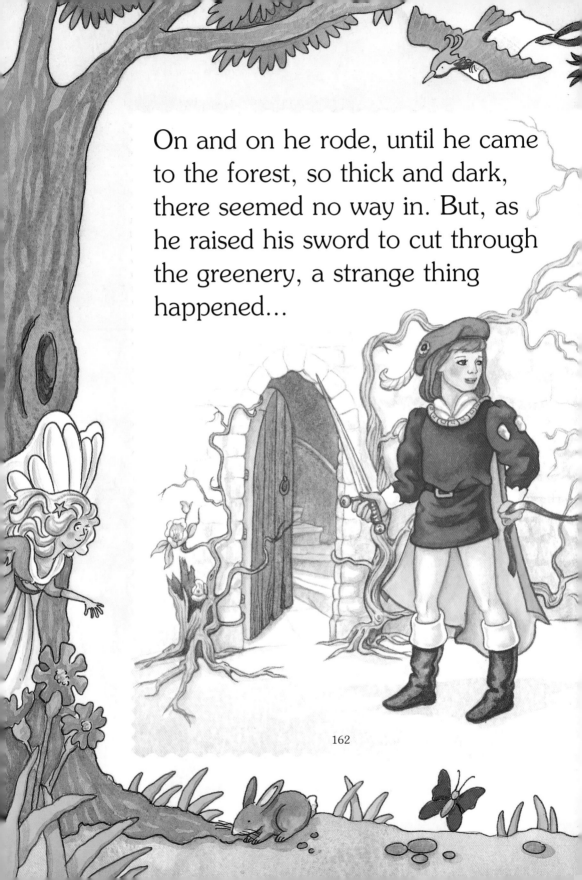

The forest of trees and bushes parted, so that he could lead his horse to the palace! Nothing had changed since the day when the evil spell of Carabos had come true…

The prince went through the little door and climbed the stairs. The last thing he expected to see was the princess, still young, still fast asleep...

She was so lovely, the prince fell in love with her at once. As he bent to kiss her, she opened her eyes and gave him a sweet smile.

165

At the same moment, the birds outside the window began to sing, the leaves rustled in the breeze, and a bell sounded in the kitchen. The long sleep was over!

The prince had shown that love and courage could triumph over the worst evil! And the princess?

She knew he was the sweetheart she had always dreamed of marrying, one day.

TWO LITTLE DUCKS

Two little ducks that I once knew,
Fat ducks, skinny ducks,
There were two.

But the one little duck
With the feathers on his back,
He led the other
With a quack, quack, quack.

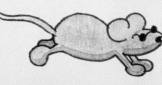

THREE BLIND MICE

Three blind mice, three blind mice,
See how they run, see how they run!
They all ran after the farmer's wife,

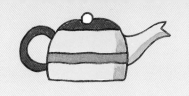

Who cut off their tails
With the carving knife,
Did you ever see
Such a thing in your life,
As three blind mice?

171

TWO LITTLE DICKIE BIRDS

Two little dickie birds sitting on a wall,
One named Peter,
One named Paul.

172

Fly away, Peter!
Fly away, Paul!
Come back, Peter!
Come back, Paul!

173

JACK BE NIMBLE

Jack be nimble,
Jack be quick,
Jack jump over
The candlestick.

HIGGELDY, PIGGELDY

Higgeldy, piggeldy, my black hen,
She lays eggs for gentlemen;
Sometimes nine and sometimes ten,
Higgeldy, piggeldy, my black hen.

SIMPLE SIMON

Simple Simon met a pieman
Going to the fair;
Said Simple Simon to the pieman:
"Let me taste your ware."

Said the pieman to Simple Simon:
"Show me first your penny."
Said Simple Simon to the pieman:
"Indeed, I have not any."

177

OLD MOTHER HUBBARD

Old Mother Hubbard
Went to the cupboard,
To get her poor doggy a bone;

178

But when she got there,
The cupboard was bare,
And so the poor doggy had none!

THE GRAND OLD DUKE OF YORK

Oh, the grand old Duke of York,
He had ten thousand men;

180

He marched them up to the top of the hill,
And he marched them down again.
And when they were up, they were up,
And when they were down, they were down,
And when they were only halfway up,
They were neither up nor down.

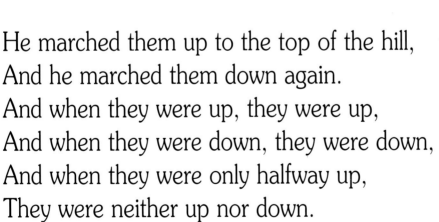

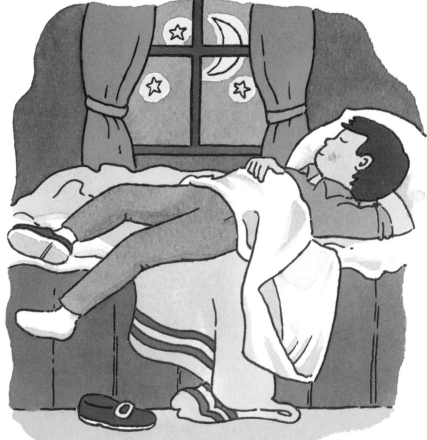

DIDDLE, DIDDLE, DUMPLING

Diddle, diddle, dumpling, my son John,
Went to bed with his trousers on;
One shoe off and one shoe on,
Diddle, diddle, dumpling, my son John.

HICKORY, DICKORY DOCK

Hickory, dickory dock,
The mouse ran up the clock.
The clock struck one,
The mouse ran down,
Hickory, dickory dock.

TO MARKET, TO MARKET

To market, to market,
To buy a fat pig,
Home again, home again,
Jiggety jig.

184

To market, to market,
To buy a fat hog,
Home again, home again,
Jiggety jog.

THERE WAS AN OLD WOMAN

There was an old woman,
Who lived in a shoe,
She had so many children
She didn't know what to do;

186

She gave them some broth,
Without any bread,
She whipped them all soundly,
And sent them to bed.

I HAD A LITTLE NUT TREE

I had a little nut tree,
Nothing would it bear
But a silver nutmeg
And a golden pear.

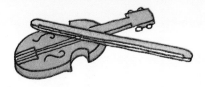

The King of Spain's daughter
Came to visit me,
And all for the sake
Of my little nut tree.

189

INDEX

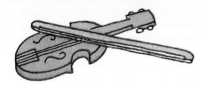

The King of Spain's daughter
Came to visit me,
And all for the sake
Of my little nut tree.

INDEX

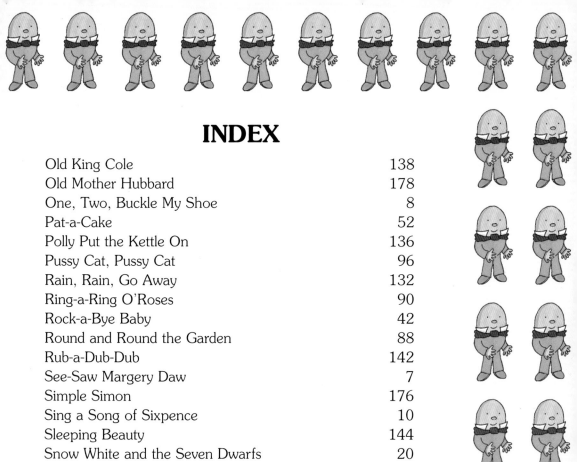

INDEX

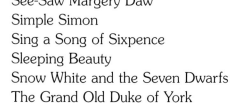

ISBN: 978-0-7097-1435-4

This edition first published 2001 by Brown Watson
The Old Mill, 76 Fleckney Road,
Kibworth Beauchamp,
Leicestershire LE8 0HG
© 2001 Brown Watson
Reprinted 2003, 2004, 2005, 2006, 2011
Printed in Malaysia